Written By: Kim Hipple
Illustrated By: Nazia Bi Bi

Let's

 *What's Next...*

The apple was Big.

Bonnie bought a basket.

The basket was Colorful.

Christian caught a caterpillar.

The caterpillar was Dancing.

Darla did some digging.

The digging was **E**asy.

Eddie took the elevator.

The elevator was Fun.

Freddie fixed his food.

The food was Gooey.

The hockey rink was Icy.

The ice tea was in a Jar.

Jack did a high jump.

Lily loves lavender lilies.

The lilies smell Magnificent.

The monkey mimicked adia.

The nut was shaped like an Oval.

The ocean was **P**retty.

Quinn found a quarter.

The quarter was Round.

Rachel collected rocks.

The rocks were Shiny.

Sophie played with Scruffy.

The trash bag was Untied.

Wally saw a wounded walrus.

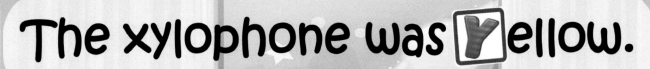
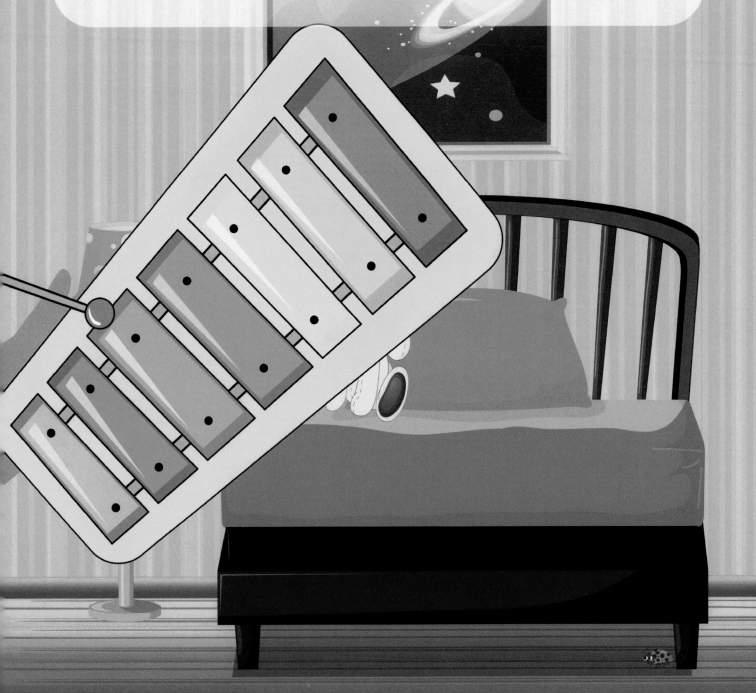

Yoland was yawning.

THE END